## About the ONCE UPON AMERICA® Series

Who is affected by the events of history? Not only the famous and powerful. Individuals from every part of society contribute a *story*—and so weave together *history*. Some of the finest storytellers bring their talents to this series of historical fiction, based on careful research and designed specifically for readers ages 7–11. These are tales of young people growing up in a young, dynamic country. Each ONCE UPON AMERICA volume shapes the reader's understanding of the people who built America and of his or her own role in our unfolding history. For history is a story that we continue to write, with a chapter for each of us beginning, "Once upon America."

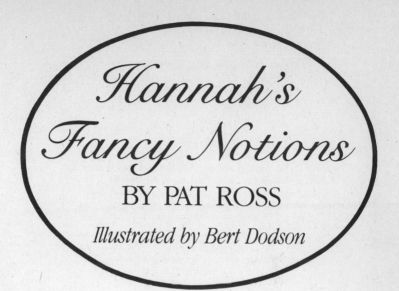

# Hannah's Fancy Notions

## BY PAT ROSS

*Illustrated by Bert Dodson*

PUFFIN BOOKS

*For Mother*

*And with thanks to Berta
and John Montgomery*

PUFFIN BOOKS

Published by the Penguin Group

Penguin Books USA Inc., 375 Hudson Street, New York, New York 10014, U.S.A.

Penguin Books Ltd, 27 Wrights Lane, London W8 5TZ, England

Penguin Books Australia Ltd, Ringwood, Victoria, Australia

Penguin Books Canada Ltd, 10 Alcorn Avenue, Toronto, Ontario, Canada M4V 3B2

Penguin Books (N.Z.) Ltd, 182–190 Wairau Road, Auckland 10, New Zealand

Penguin Books Ltd, Registered Offices: Harmondsworth, Middlesex, England

First published in the United States of America
by Viking Penguin Inc. 1988
Published in Puffin Books, 1992

20  19  18  17  16  15  14  13  12  11

LIBRARY OF CONGRESS CATALOGING-IN-PUBLICATION DATA
Ross, Pat. 1943–
Hannah's fancy notions / by Pat Ross; illustrated by Bert Dodson.
p.   cm.—(Once upon America)
Summary: When Hannah sets out to make something special for her
sister, who works to support the family, she doesn't suspect the far-
reaching consequences of her gift.
ISBN 0-14-032389-9
[1. Sisters—Fiction.   2. Business enterprises—Fiction.]
I. Dodson, Bert, ill.   II. Title.   III. Series.
[PZ7.R71973Han  1992]    [Fic]—dc20    92-20286

Printed in the United States of America
Set in Garamond No. 3

# Contents

# Hannah's Fancy Notions

# A Distant Whistle

The wind across the meadow always picks up in the late afternoon. Hannah chooses that time to break from her chores and sit on the porch.

The wind begins as a secretive rustling in the treetops on the other side of the broad clover field. Hannah takes a deep breath and holds it, waiting for the familiar wind to gather courage and then sweep boldly across the meadow, rippling the clover like ocean waves. Then, as if from nowhere, a cool breeze slaps Hannah's cheek and startles her. At the same time, a shrill little cry from the woodpile reminds Hannah that you cannot take your eyes off a baby, not even for the wind.

Just in time, Hannah finds Maggie trying to climb

the logs that Papa has cut and carefully stacked for winter. Maggie is pleased with her newfound game. Hannah is grateful that her baby sister has not set off an avalanche. It would be Maggie's fault, but Hannah would get the blame!

As usual, Maggie spent her day getting into mischief. She painted a wall with berry jam, rubbed her hair with honey, and gave the last of their milk to a strange wandering cat. Then she knocked over a butter churn, ate two buttons that Hannah was sewing on Papa's work shirt, hid the scissors, and wet their warmest blanket.

"I am not ready for motherhood," sighs Hannah in frustration. "And I am certainly not ready for the likes of Maggie!"

There are five children in Hannah's family, all daughters, and although on a day such as this one Hannah certainly feels like the eldest, she is not. Rebecca is the eldest, but she is away most of the time, leaving Hannah in charge. Nora and Sadie are twins, and they are six. Then, of course, there is Maggie, the baby, who has just begun to walk and talk and set Hannah crazy.

Suddenly Hannah realizes it is growing late. She sends the twins in search of their shoes—which always seem to be lost.

"With four shoes the very same color, style, and size, you'd think we could find at least one!" Hannah cries, knowing they must find all four. Sadie and Nora pay no attention to Hannah, who wants them dressed properly today because it is Friday, a special day. But soon she realizes that the twins will wind up barefoot and bonnetless as usual.

In the distance, a whistle calls across the thick clover field from town. At first Hannah thinks it is only the wind playing tricks. But as the sound grows bolder for the second and then the third time, Hannah is sure that the low and faraway sound is the early evening whistle. It is a welcome signal to everyone within earshot that another day has passed and evening is upon them. And if the evening stagecoach from Lowell is on time, it is also a signal that weary coach passengers are waiting to be met. This is what Hannah has looked forward to all week long.

Hannah is ready to meet the Friday stagecoach. It has been a long trip for the good-natured traveler who waits at the depot for them, and Hannah wants everyone to look neat, clean, and well-behaved. Unfortunately, neatness, cleanliness, and good behavior are the farthest things from the minds of her three charges!

By the third whistle, the twins have bolted through the door and are halfway across the field to the stage-

coach depot, looking and acting like wild ragamuffins. Hannah lifts Maggie onto her shoulders and calls for Papa.

Papa no longer goes with them to meet the Friday coach. Once Papa was jolly and ready to take on anybody in a good footrace across that same field. But the winter before, their mother fell ill with a sudden fever one night after dinner. By the morning, she had died. Since then, Papa has lost his energy and his sparkle. Thinking of Mama makes Hannah sad, but it has not changed her the way it has changed Papa.

Hannah pushes thoughts of her mother to a silent place in her mind. She does not wish to think of Mama now. It would not be fair to let sadness spoil a Friday.

# *Papa's Cat Tale*

"Papa, the baby and I are ready," Hannah calls toward the shed behind the house where Papa spends his days lately. It has been such a long time since Papa went with them to the depot, but Hannah never stops asking him, and she never stops hoping.

A paperhanger by trade, Papa takes jobs in the fine homes outside of Boston. That is, he works when his back does not ache from the job before. These days, he seems to ache more and work less. More often than not, the money tin is empty. That is why Rebecca, the eldest, has taken a factory job in the mill town of Lowell, Massachusetts, a two-hour coach ride from their home.

Rebecca leaves every Monday before anyone else in the family has risen. The stagecoach on the Lowell route is one of the first through. It picks up Rebecca and the other girls who work in factory towns during the week. There they live in run-down boarding-houses, counting the days till they can return to their homes for a visit—if only for a day. But the pay—as much as three dollars a week—makes it worth it.

Most of the factories are kept running around the clock, seven days a week. And many of the factory workers practically live at their hard and thankless jobs, dreaming only of sleep and a good hot meal. But Rebecca has been lucky. Soon after she began working six days a week, a fire in one building left her factory short of machines and long on workers. The factory has cut back the work week (and, of course, the pay!) for the women and children while they re-build. And everyone knows that soon they all must return to longer days and even longer weeks. Hannah knows that Rebecca will be lost to her for weeks at a time then. So she will enjoy Fridays while she can.

Hannah finds Papa in the shed. He seems to be sorting bits and pieces of leftover wallpaper. But his hair is flat on one side and Hannah guesses that he's been napping most of the afternoon. She glances over at a pile of work rags. The funny bumps of wallpaper paste on them have stiffened with age. It's easy to make out a deep dent in the pile the same size as Papa's body. Hannah is sure if she places her hand on that spot, it will still be warm from his nap.

"The whistle, Papa," Hannah tells Papa, who seems groggy and unsure of the time. "Rebecca will be in."

"Goodness," declares Papa. "I must have been working so hard I plum missed the whistle."

"You missed all three whistles," scolds Hannah. "And I suppose you'll miss meeting Rebecca again, too."

"You're a capable girl, Hannah," says Papa, patting Hannah's cheek and smiling down at Maggie, who is content with her doll. "You can bring Rebecca and the others home."

Hannah is tired of being a capable girl! When Mama died, Rebecca took over, and that seemed natural. Rebecca is so much like Mama that there are times when Hannah catches herself saying *Mama* when she means *Rebecca*. Rebecca did everything Mama did, and Hannah was happy to help her with the baby and with the willful twins. Together they finished all the chores and had time for all the things that Hannah liked to think up. One weekend they made potato faces out of peeled potatoes and bits of kitchen greens and stalks from the garden. Over the winter, Rebecca taught them to piece a quilt using colorful scraps that Hannah collected from neighbors' scrap bags. With Rebecca in charge, Hannah felt safe and carefree.

But everything changed when Rebecca left to work in Lowell. Hannah knows how to cook, so no one starves. She tries to keep the children neat and clean and makes sure they get to bed on time. But all the while she is giving baths or collecting eggs for breakfast, she wishes Rebecca were in charge. There is no time left for making things or having fun, and Hannah feels tired and cranky much of the time. When she feels this way, she just can't help blaming Papa.

"Run along," says Papa. "Give me a chance to work the kinks out of my aching back. There's a new job near Boston next week, and I'm hoping to be on it." Hannah knows that Papa means well, but she has heard all this before.

When Mama was alive, Papa's whistling was the first thing they heard in the morning. His scratchy beard rubbed their tender faces when he kissed them each good-bye, then headed off in the wagon for some papering job near Boston. At night when they saw Papa's wagon bumping up the road, Mama, Maggie, Rebecca, Hannah, Nora, and Sadie all ran to meet him, eager for a tale of some fine house near Boston which he would tell over dinner.

11

Hannah used to believe anything Papa told them about life in the fine houses where he worked, even if his stories seemed a bit too incredible to be true, even for the rich. Her favorite story was about the family cat who was served tea.

"Now I wouldn't have known and wouldn't have ever believed such a thing if I hadn't been there, right there in the parlor during teatime." Hannah remembers how Papa made such grand statements, his sharp dark eyes looking to each of them for a reaction.

Hannah can hear her father go on and on: "I was minding my business, papering the parlor in a pattern all filled with strange and beautiful birds in flight, trying to match each bird with its rightful tail on the next piece, when I noticed a pampered-looking cat eyeing the birds, especially the ones up high near me. This cat pranced back and forth, looking grand and treating me like some intruder. Then, all of a sudden, I heard a bell, and so did his majesty. In no time, this cat had leapt right onto the cushion of the most elegant chair in the room. Red plush, I believe. I kept my eyes on my work, but the eyes in the back of my head saw everything when a maid rustled into the room with a tray of tea and biscuits. Well, I thought this was a friendly thing to do for a wallpaper hanger

12

who was parched and hungry. So I started down my ladder."

Hannah remembers how everyone giggled at the thought of Papa coming down for tea, and how Papa grew even more dramatic as his story took them in so totally.

"But I stopped halfway down," Papa had gone on, "when I saw that maid place a silver tray right in front of that pampered cat, who appeared to expect nothing less. Then without a word, the maid poured the cat one cup of tea with two sugars and a generous splash of cream. While he was waiting for his tea to cool, she placed a biscuit on a china plate with enough jam for two *people*. And then she left the parlor."

At this point, Papa returned to his dinner, leaving everyone impatient for the final chapter.

"Well, *then* what?" they cried and pleaded to know.

"Why, don't you know?' asked Papa, as though they ought to know the rest. "I did what any self-respecting paperhanger would do. I let the cat have my ladder to paper a few birds. And, in exchange, he gave me his biscuit and tea, which I ate and drank on that elegant plush chair."

Papa no longer told wonderful stories of fine houses or of anything else for that matter. He was still kind and good, and Hannah still loved him. But everything was different, and Papa was the most different of all.

"Run along," Papa repeats, startling Hannah back from the past. He doesn't give her a chance to beg him one more time. He just kisses little Maggie on the head and sends them on their way to fetch Rebecca.

# A Poor
# Working Girl

Hannah is late as usual—because of everyone else. The stagecoach is in, and Rebecca is waving to them. Rebecca is only a tiny figure in the distance, but Maggie sees her, too, and begins to squirm in Hannah's arms.

Rebecca looks old enough to be the mother of all of them, even Hannah, who is nearly ten. Yet Rebecca is just turning fifteen. She is taller than most women twice her age, taller now than Mama was when she died.

Today Rebecca is wearing their mother's best dress— the pretty dark one with the lace collar and tiny buttons. A bow under her chin is tied tight to keep her

15

hat on during the long ride. It hardly moves when she leans over to pick up Maggie, who is reaching out her arms. The twins are busy exploring the stagecoach, which lays over for an hour before heading on.

The other working girls who have arrived with Rebecca wait shyly near the driver. Despite the long ride, their dresses are still fresh-looking. Hannah can tell that they are also brand-new. The girls usually save their new and best clothes for the trip home. All week long these clothes have been packed safely away, saved for the journey. Their everyday dresses, soiled and ripped by the factory machines, are tucked away in sacks and satchels, secure with bits of rope and twine. Most of the girls buy stylish city clothes with part of their pay. But Rebecca brings home every penny.

"Oh, Rebecca," says Hannah. "On Monday mornings when you leave, you're my sister. On Fridays, you've become some grown-up lady!"

"Well, I don't *feel* very grown up," Rebecca replies without hesitation. "People always think I'm so much older, and I just want to tell them: 'Pardon me, but you've mistaken me for a grown-up.'"

"I'm sorry I've mistaken you for a grown-up," Hannah teases.

"Even though I'm just a poor working girl, I do try to be a lady," Rebecca confides to Hannah proudly.

"On the ride home, sometimes I pretend that I am a lady from one of Papa's fine houses outside of Boston. No one can tell that the dress I wear was made by Mama and not bought in some city store. And I make sure that I push my raggedy sack under my skirt so you can't see plain as day that I am most surely a poor working girl with a week's pay to my name stuffed deep in my pocket."

A cart passes noisily by and nearly runs over Rebecca's sack. Tied tight with twine from home, the sack holds a calico dress mended in five places, a useful apron to keep her clean, and just enough for five days away from home. The cart is piled high with trunks and luggage belonging to passengers who are not mill girls. Hannah is sure the large black trunks are filled with splendid party gowns and many pairs of shoes. On top of the trunks, dark and plain hatboxes of different sizes are piled high and wobbly.

"Imagine having a special box just for your hat!" declares Rebecca, who is looking, too. "I can't imagine anything more wonderful!"

Suddenly Hannah wishes Rebecca had a hatbox at least. Her sister deserves something better than a poor girl's luggage.

Crossing the field for home, with Rebecca's burlap sack under her arm, Hannah finds herself envying

Rebecca. She sometimes wishes she were the one to travel to a place like Lowell and work like a grown-up. Chopping greens to make soup, scolding two naughty girls, and having a baby wet your lap while your father sleeps his days away certainly is tiresome. In the city, Hannah's sure, she would meet interesting people and no damp-bottomed babies! Surely she would find a job more exciting than collecting eggs from nervous hens.

"I envy you, Hannah," says Rebecca, breaking into Hannah's thoughts about life in the city. "Each week I count the days from Monday till Friday, and Friday never comes fast enough. On Sunday nights, I twist and turn, waiting for daybreak. And I cannot even bring myself to think about working six days straight when the factory's back to full labor."

Hannah stirs every Monday morning, even though Rebecca is as quiet as she is gentle. She always hears Rebecca stuffing clothes in her burlap sack, taking her one-way fare from the money tin, then slipping silently away from them. She had no idea that it might be more difficult for Rebecca than it is for her, until now.

"I liked it when you were home, Becca. I'm not very good at Mama's job, and I miss you." Hannah wonders if they will ever go back to the way things were.

"I like Mama's job, Hannah. I love the girls, especially little Maggie. And you, Hannah, you are so quick and clever that the work seems joyful when we do it together."

"Papa says I am *capable!*" Hannah moans.

"But that is true, too!" Rebecca exclaims. "Cleverness alone can't make good ideas happen. You are capable as well, Hannah. As for me, I do the dull things well, and somehow manage to take pride in them. I miss making soup and mending Papa's collars so they look like new. And then you were always there to bring something unexpected to the routine of the day. That is your special gift. Why, remember the time . . ."

She reminds Hannah of a day many months before when the weather was wet and gray and the children were ill-humored. Papa had come home very late from one of his last jobs, dropped a pile of scrap wood and wallpaper in the corner of the kitchen, and gone to bed. All day long, no one noticed the rather ordinary-looking pile, until Hannah tripped over it.

"I tripped over the idea!" cries Hannah, remembering.

The pile was mostly junk—things that Papa would eventually throw away. But among the junk were thin boards and several lengths of wood just right for

19

building something small, plus five rolls of rejected wallpaper that had been printed crooked.

That afternoon, when the twins whined that there was nothing to do, Rebecca rocked little Maggie, and Hannah sorted through the pile while an idea took form. Soon she had just enough small pieces assembled on the kitchen table to begin.

On a piece of paper Hannah drew a box, then a triangle on that box, then squares in the box. At that point, everyone was watching. "A house!" Sadie cried, the first to recognize Hannah's drawing. "A dollhouse," Hannah declared. "Our dollhouse. Or it will be soon enough."

All afternoon the four of them hammered and glued their little dollhouse. It was plain and simple, but it was big enough for all of them to work on. When the last nail was hammered, it was time to make that dollhouse beautiful.

The crooked wallpaper would be perfect. It was yellow and green with great white swans holding a basket of fruit. Because the pattern was printed crooked, the swans ran off the side of the sheets, losing a head or a tail in ridiculous ways that made everyone giggle. Such paper was of no use to the fine homes outside of Boston, but it had a use that day.

If Hannah cut the design in just the right way, the

swans looked straight and proud, so she did the cutting. Rebecca was in charge of the pasting. The twins smoothed the paper down and wiped up the paste drippings. Soon their small dollhouse was covered with swans, inside and out. It was not plain anymore.

For the next week, no one had to be asked to help with the chores. Sadie learned to dust and Nora could put away dishes without dropping a single one. Everyone wanted to finish quickly so there would be plenty of time to work on that house.

The four of them lifted their swan house onto the table, where it looked more lived-in every day. Once the papering was finished, there was furniture to make— a tiny table and chairs made from twigs, bright rugs to knit from leftover yarn, and miniature pictures to draw for the walls. Even Papa could not resist Hannah's house. One night he made shutters for every window and a modest porch by the front door.

"We never made people for our house," says Hannah. "I don't think we wanted anyone else to live there, even if we could be in charge of who they were. I guess I liked it that way."

Hannah shifts the weight of Rebecca's sack as they head down the last stretch of field for home.

# Scraps
## of Pretty Paper

Rebecca's fifteenth birthday is tomorrow, Sunday. Since there is never an extra penny in the money tin, Hannah will make Rebecca a special gift—but what? The twins wind a daisy chain and Maggie picks the heads off the daisies when the twins look the other way.

Hannah decides to look for Papa in the shed. She must make sure he hasn't forgotten Rebecca's birthday. When she pushes open the creaky door, the sun bursts in from behind her and brightens the tiny space.

The first thing Hannah notices is Papa's work cloths. They are folded more neatly than she remembered.

Rolls and half-rolls, bits and odd scraps of wallpaper are all tied up neatly, then tucked in cubbyholes for safekeeping. Papa's work room used to be a mess, so it seems that he *has* been sorting wallpaper after all! Right away, Hannah realizes he has saved every last piece.

As strange as it may seem, not one room in the house has ever been wallpapered. There is simply never enough left over to wallpaper an entire room, except for the crooked swan paper, which would have made them dizzy. So Hannah finds herself looking at the wallpaper as though seeing it for the very first time.

Hannah begins to undo Papa's neat rolls. The first wallpaper has a long-tailed cockatoo flying across yards of twisting vines, all bright and proud. Then Hannah comes to rolls of wild beasts printed boldly. A camel is looking smug. A hippopotamus is grazing. Hannah is feeling more at home when she unrolls a paper printed with familiar brown squirrels.

Careful to be as neat as Papa, Hannah unrolls one piece after another. There are wallpapers filled with leaves—some star-shaped and graceful—a field of for-get-me-nots, a bowl of ripe fruit too perfect to look real. Finally Hannah finds a favorite wallpaper—huge blooming roses that would make a room into a garden!

No wonder Papa has saved even the smallest piece.

A pair of scissors lying on the table is within reach. Not wishing to spoil a single piece, Hannah begins to fold and cut a small piece, working carefully. Soon she has made a paper doll, plain on one side and filled with flowers on the other. She will paint a person on the plain side . . .

"But Rebecca is too old for paper dolls," she says out loud. So she makes another so that there is a doll for each twin.

Some of the wallpaper is very stiff, so Hannah sews two round pieces together and stuffs the circle with sawdust. She tosses the colorful ball into the air. It's the perfect gift for Maggie, but not for Rebecca.

If the wallpaper were pieces of cloth, Hannah would start a quilt for Rebecca that instant. "But what can anyone do with bits of wallpaper?" she says louder now, angry and discouraged.

"That's what I asked myself when I rolled them up and put them away," says Papa, startling Hannah by his presence. "I should have thrown them away like a sensible man."

"Why did you bother?" asks Hannah.

"Your mother saved everything. She said you never know when something might come in handy." And that seemed to say it all.

"Help me think of something for Rebecca's birthday," Hannah begs Papa.

"Ah, a thoughtful sister, a poor papa, and Hannah's dreams . . ." Papa sounds discouraged already.

Suddenly Hannah thinks of the tattered sack that Rebecca carries on the train. Then she remembers the hatboxes belonging to fine ladies who travel.

"A hatbox!" she cries. "We'll make Rebecca a pretty hatbox!"

"But Rebecca has only one hat and she wears it," says Papa firmly. "Although you are a capable girl, sometimes you waste your time with dreams and useless things. Rebecca is a poor working girl. She has no need for a fancy hatbox."

"Then we'll make something bigger and stronger than a hatbox," declares Hannah, undaunted. "There are bandboxes for men's collars and bandboxes for ladies' waistbands. There are boxes of all sizes. I have seen them at the depot. So we can make a box that is just right for a working girl. A box to hold her clothes."

Papa is not up to an argument, so he just shakes his head and leaves the shed to Hannah. "Fancy notions . . ." she hears him mutter.

Hannah spends the rest of the afternoon cutting out pieces of strong cardboard, inventing her bandbox. When she thinks the pieces are the right size and shape, she pastes them together. At the end of the afternoon, she has a box that is too tall and too skinny, a lopsided box that topples over, and a stubborn box that keeps splitting its pasted seams.

Just before dinner, Hannah hears Rebecca leave the house and head toward the shed. Quickly she shoves her miserable-looking failures under the table and covers them with a cloth stiffened with paste.

Now Hannah must help Rebecca dig potatoes for dinner. Hannah thinks it is strange the way those potatoes live under the cold earth and see the daylight only long enough to be scrubbed clean before they meet their fate in some equally dark oven. Concentrating on potatoes helps her to forget the boxes.

"One more day," Rebecca sighs, brushing the earth off her potatoes.

"Do you hate it?" asks Hannah. "I never even thought about your hating it so much."

"Oh, I don't hate it, but I don't like working in some factory much either. They make us work so long and hard, Hannah! Sometimes, if we need a little extra money, I work into the night. The work itself is not so hard, just threading a weaving machine for me. But it's cold in the winter and sweltering hot in the summer, and no one seems to care. It's harder on the older women."

"Do they beat you?" asks Hannah, her imagination taking off. Up until this time she has never given much thought to what Rebecca's life is like away from home.

"No, not in my factory," says Rebecca. "But I've heard rumors that some do."

"What about Mrs. Hathaway's? Don't you like living at Mrs. Hathaway's?" Hannah wants to know, suddenly curious about all of Rebecca's life away from her. Mrs. Hathaway runs the boardinghouse where Rebecca lives during the week. She has imagined Mrs. Hathaway as a kind and loving mother for the working girls, someone who cooks good hot meals and tucks them in bed at night.

"Mrs. Hathaway doesn't pay much attention to us. She's more interested in our pay at the end of the week. On Fridays she's as nice as can be, always asking what time we'll be in on Monday so she'll know how long our room is free to let. But her cooking is good enough and no one starves. I do have my friends, other girls from the factory mostly, and we sit up and talk when we're not too tired. We talk a lot about our families and how we'd rather be home, like you are. It's not awful, Hannah, it's just not home." Rebecca's voice grows thin and distant. Somehow Hannah knows what is coming.

"And now there is talk of returning to six days in a matter of weeks. No more Fridays. But," Rebecca brightens, "we still have tomorrow together!"

They celebrate Rebecca's birthday the next night after dinner. Papa is jolly for a moment when he brings in the cake. Rebecca wears the daisy chain and exclaims over the paper dolls for the twins and Maggie's new ball, even though Hannah has nothing for her.

Hannah feels sad and discouraged. She had wanted to give Rebecca something special, but ended up with failures instead.

Rebecca will leave tomorrow when the morning whistle blows. Knowing now what Rebecca faces makes it all the harder to let her go.

# *Plain and Fancy*

Rebecca's loss is felt by Hannah even more during the week that follows. Maggie has taken sick with a fever and needs Hannah constantly. On Wednesday, the twins play secretly and quietly in the flour bin and pretend they are snowpeople. It takes Hannah all afternoon to sweep up the snow. Then she dusts off the twins and gives them a good sponging-down in the washtub. Papa manages to be out of sight most of Hannah's troublesome day.

Finally, Maggie is better and the twins, worn out from their naughty play, nap soundly. In fact, they are sleeping so contentedly beneath Papa and Mama's large quilt that Hannah decides to take Maggie out for some air. The day is mild and Hannah is sure Rebecca would recommend fresh air.

The door to the shed is banging in the breeze. Someone has forgotten to latch it. With Maggie balanced on her hip, Hannah makes her way across the yard. She hesitates at the door, then decides to enter.

Hannah has not been back to the shed since her disappointing day with the cardboard boxes. Suddenly she is curious to see if they have *all* popped their pasted seams and are lying flat and useless on the floor where she left them.

Beneath the stiff cloth that she flung over the boxes, she can see their bulging shapes. So they are still standing! Now she will just have to break them down and throw them away. She sits Maggie on the soft pile of work cloths and kneels by the table. A finger of sunshine touches the dried paint drips on the cloth. It reminds her of some strange and awful skin, nearly lifelike. Suddenly, Hannah wants to get this over with! She tosses back the cloth.

But something magical has happened. Three wonderful boxes stand in the places of the failures! They are straight and sturdy, their seams are sewn with heavy thread, and their tops fit securely. Hannah has never believed in fairies and elves, but perhaps she has been wrong not to! Only an elf with skill and

32

persistence and hours to spare could have copied Hannah's failed boxes and come up with such perfect ones. Only an elf . . . or Papa.

"Papa!" cries Hannah. "Oh, Papa, where are you?" She heads for the yard, her heart racing now with the fear she might be wrong.

Papa is greasing the axles of their wagon, which has been creaking like a rusty hinge now for months. Just by the way he smiles and looks proud of himself, Hannah knows Papa is the bandbox elf. She jumps into his arms with such force that they are both startled and pleased by this sudden gesture.

"You did it, Papa! You did it!"

"I didn't want to let you down again," Papa replies shyly. "You and Rebecca. Anyway, I just improved on your good idea."

"My good idea needed help," says Hannah, modestly.

"Well, what next?" Papa is eager now. "I guess you might say I'm at your service. That is, if you need me."

"Papa, I've always needed you," says Hannah, her voice so soft and true that her words could not be doubted.

For the first time in a year, Hannah and Papa find themselves talking and laughing like old friends—and

now partners. For the rest of the afternoon and throughout the next day, they work on perfecting their traveling box for Rebecca.

Sewing holds the boxes together far better than paste, so Papa shows Hannah how to use a cobbler's needle and heavy thread. Finally they stand back to admire their fine finished boxes, the best of which will become Rebecca's.

"They are strong, Papa," says Hannah. "But they are so very plain."

"Well, some folks like them plain," states Papa matter-of-factly.

"But some folks like them fancy," replies Hannah brightly. "And I know how to fancy them, Papa! I know just what will make them right!"

Hannah points to the pile of Papa's neatly folded pieces and rolls of wallpaper in the cubbyholes. Mama was right about saved things coming in handy. The wonderful wallpaper will be just right to make a plain box fancy.

Quickly, Hannah and Papa undo part of a roll—tossed bouquets of lilies. That will certainly do.

Hannah chooses the cardboard box she likes the least to cover first, just in case it doesn't turn out on the first try. To cover it, she uses the lily paper. It is a pretty enough paper, but certainly not her favorite.

She mixes the paste, and Papa does most of the cutting and pasting. He works quickly and skillfully the way a paperhanger would. There is a fold here and a tuck there, but hardly anyone would notice such imperfections.

The inside looks plain and rough, so Papa cuts a lining of newsprint. "No one sees inside," he reasons, happy to have thought of a lining so smart and thrifty.

On the second box, Papa mixes the paste and Hannah learns to measure and cut the pieces. Together they do the pasting. This box has a bowl of fruit on both sides and it is very pleasing, and almost perfect. Now it is Hannah's turn to cover the third box herself—the one for Rebecca. And that one must be the very best.

Hannah chooses her favorite wallpaper—enormous red roses in full bloom, twisting their way through a trellis. Roses are Rebecca's favorite flower.

"My, but you are fast and handy!" declares Papa as he watches Hannah cut the paper to size. Just knowing that Papa is proud makes Hannah work without one mistake. Soon the box is finished, and it is the very best one.

"But how will Rebecca carry it easily?" asks Papa, holding Hannah's box high for them to admire. Hannah disappears into the house and returns with Mama's sewing things. Inside a painted basket, faded and softened with years, she and Papa find yards and yards of ribbon and trim. Luckily for them, Mama saved everything.

They choose a strong green ribbon to wind around the box and over the lid. It seems fitting that the ribbon was left over from one of Mama's favorite dresses.

The bandbox is finished. It sits high on a shelf in the house for the rest of the week, to be protected and admired. Every time Hannah looks up, she can see Rebecca dressed like Mama, with a fancy box on her arm.

They celebrate Rebecca's birthday for the second time. She is weary from her long week and more quiet than usual, but the surprise cheers her. When she sees the real reason for the occasion—Hannah's special gift—she is happy in a way that brings back feelings from the past, when life seemed filled with surprises.

"Oh, Hannah, now I *am* a real lady," she declares. "No one will have a bandbox to match this one. Just wait till everyone sees my gift. This is the first time I have not dreaded Monday!"

Rebecca is not up to her usual number of chores over the weekend. She leaves the baking to Hannah while she reads to the girls. That's the way it was before she went off to work in Lowell.

This weekend, Hannah has rounded up small pieces of newsprint left over from the bandbox linings. Together she and Rebecca search for news stories with words simple enough for Sadie and Nora to read.

"Here's one," Rebecca says to the twins, smiling. "BULL RUNS WILD AND TRAMPLES GARDEN. Some of the words are hard, but you can figure out the easy ones and we'll help with the rest."

But Sadie and Nora are in no mood to struggle through a reading lesson. "*You* read about the bad bull!" they shout.

Rebecca studies the small print and begins: "Early Monday morning, a bull belonging to Joshua Hinson and known to be of disagreeable disposition broke through a fence belonging to Rufus Bosworth. The bull located the rose garden and began trampling the flowers and vines."

Sadie and Nora begin stomping and snorting like Mr. Hinson's bull.

"Mr. Bosworth was sleeping, but Mrs. Bosworth, who was in the kitchen, began to shout at the bull and wave her best broom from the protection of the porch. The Hinson bull charged the porch and Mrs. Bosworth."

Now Hannah and Rebecca are laughing so hard, Rebecca can barely see the tiny type.

She goes on, stifling a hiccup. "The porch sustained minor damage. Mrs. Bosworth was treated by Dr. Matthew Duxbury for a resulting nervous disorder. Mr. Hinson has offered to pay for all damage, and apologized to Mrs. Bosworth, who has taken to her bed over the incident."

"That was a good story," Sadie says.

"I liked the bull," Nora adds.

"Bad bull!" cries Maggie, in a small scolding voice, so sharp and clear that they are all quite startled.

"Maggie's not a baby anymore," says Rebecca wistfully. "We have all grown up too quickly."

Her words stab at Hannah's heart. It's not fair that Rebecca should have to leave again. She goes to find Papa to tell him so.

Papa is sitting under a tree, gazing toward Boston. His new job will be starting soon. Surely then Rebecca can stay home forever.

His eyes are empty when Hannah addresses him. As though he already knows what is on her mind, he nods. Then: "They took someone else for the job, Hannah. They won't be needing me. But something will surely turn up soon. I am just down on my luck."

Hannah hopes he is right.

On Monday morning, Rebecca rises as usual. She is quiet as a leaf dropping on an airless day. When she slips out the door, Hannah sees in the narrowing shadows a lady with a fancy bandbox on her arm.

# *A Contest*
# *with the Wind*

Memories of Mama push their way into Hannah's thoughts now, escaping the silent place that she has tucked them these many weeks. When she has Rebecca near or promising a quick return, Hannah does not miss Mama with the same sadness. Now that Rebecca may soon be lost to her in a different way, Hannah finally allows herself to miss them both.

Mama was gentle and cheerful, and there is not a day that Hannah does not wonder how things might have been. . . . She likes to remember the times that they spent together, just the two of them, when the other girls were working or playing someplace else. She likes to remember the chilly day that they washed the sheets—those heavy wet sheets that seemed to weigh more than Papa!

Soon their hands were sore and red from washing and wringing. The day was cold and windy, but the sun was strong and warm. Mama said those sheets would be bleached white as angels and freshened sweet by the clean air. Mama always had a way of seeing the bright side of a dismal job. So they made sure Maggie was sleeping soundly, and then they carried the sheets into the yard.

The wind slapped Hannah and Mama hard and banged the door behind them. But the sun seemed on fire and it made them forget the cold. Together Mama and Hannah pulled the first sheet from the laundry basket. In the wind it fought them, slapping and twisting. It finally took five strong clothespins to keep the first sheet in place on the line. "There!" cried Mama over the blustery air, feeling victorious and making Hannah feel the same way.

The second and third sheets were soon hung. The job seemed to Hannah to be getting easier. Then, suddenly, the wind picked up speed and changed direction, as though to fool them. One pin flew across the yard, then another and another. Soon Hannah and Mama were chasing pins and wrestling sheets. It was a contest with the wind.

43

Those wet sheets too soon took the side of the wind. They flew at Hannah and Mama and slapped them, all cold and stiff. Again and again, Hannah and Mama tried to show those sheets who was boss. Suddenly the slapping and wrestling with sheets seemed very funny to both of them. The sun was beaming down, the wind was lashing fiercely, and Hannah and Mama were just laughing and laughing at the silliness of it all.

As they turned to put extra clothespins on the last sheet, it flew off the line like a great white sail and went floating across the yard and high into the sky. Hannah's face was wet with tears of laughter as their sheet sailed down the road, too fast and too high to be caught.

Mama wrapped her arms around Hannah's shoulders, as they watched their sheet fly away. "Well, I guess someone will sleep on a bare bed tonight," she declared matter-of-factly, knowing full well there were no extra sheets. Then they unpinned the other sheets and together carried the damp laundry back into the house, where they fixed hot tea.

Whenever Hannah thinks of Mama, she thinks of their laundry day together, and she feels Mama's presence like a sweet ghost.

# A Bandbox
## Just Like Rebecca's

When Rebecca arrives next Friday, three girls who work with her in Lowell call to Hannah from the stagecoach. For the first time in many Fridays, Hannah is there on time, only because she has made the twins stay behind with Papa.

"Hannah, oh Hannah!" one of the girls calls eagerly. "I must have a bandbox just like Rebecca's!"

"Hannah, please make one for me, too," calls another. "One with flowers and vines."

"I'll settle for something that's even half as nice as Rebecca's bandbox if I can have it right away," yet another cries. She holds up a ragged sack. "I'll be glad to carry anything but *this!*"

When they are halfway home, Rebecca holds out fifteen cents for Hannah.

"They said they'd *pay*," she declares, "so I accepted for you."

Hannah is both surprised and pleased that Rebecca has been so bold.

When they tell Papa he wastes no time making new cardboard forms—four, just in case one is not perfect. All day Sunday, Hannah and Papa make bandboxes. The twins soon learn to mix paste without getting it in their hair. Maggie plays with the scraps. Rebecca is content to keep the house in order and give advice when it is needed, which is often.

On Monday morning, Papa helps Rebecca carry the bandboxes to the depot. They have made them so that they nest one inside the other. Rebecca's friends are thrilled. They leave their old sacks by the side of the road, and go off with brand new bandboxes on their arms. Papa heads home, and they think that is that. But they are wrong.

On Friday, Rebecca arrives home with orders for not three, but *nine* more boxes!

"Hannah," says Rebecca, "you cannot imagine the stir your boxes have caused at Mrs. Hathaway's. It seems that everyone wants a bandbox. Even Mrs. Hathaway is suggesting in a rather bold fashion that I might just find a spare one for her—offering no payment, mind you."

During the week, while Rebecca is away, Hannah and Papa make bandboxes for the working girls at Mrs. Hathaway's. Papa smiles now while he works, and he teases the girls at dinner the way he used to. Hannah sometimes forgets to make the beds, and there is a thin layer of dust on the cupboard, but no one complains.

Soon they run out of newsprint for lining. "Now what?" Hannah wants to know.

Papa leaves for town with the first boxes they made, the ones that were nice but not quite perfect. He returns with a stack of newspapers, a dozen eggs, a loaf of warm bread, and a paper flower for Hannah's hair. The women in town were eager to trade their goods for those boxes, and Papa even had orders for more.

"Mr. Higgins wants one for each daughter," Papa says. Hannah remembers that Mr. Higgins has five daughters and some of the finest beef cattle around. They will receive tasty payment for their time and trouble.

Rebecca returns to Lowell with three stacks of perfect boxes. The stagecoach driver complains and asks for payment for extra luggage. What he wants is a bandbox—something in red for his wife.

Rebecca returns home with orders for more, and more, and more. Now that everyone at Mrs. Hathaway's has a bandbox (except Mrs. Hathaway, who is hinting louder than ever), other working girls in town and at the factory have seen them. The orders pour in, faster than Hannah and Papa can make them. And the orders continue as easy as that.

Soon the wallpaper supply is running dangerously low. All the flowered patterns have been used up. When Hannah checks the money tin, she is surprised to find it full, full enough to buy more wallpaper with plenty left over. Papa knows his fellow tradesmen will be happy to part with their half-rolls and scraps for a reasonable price. He is quick and always gets the paper for the best price.

In less than a month, Papa and Hannah and Rebecca cannot carry the boxes to the depot without Papa's wagon.

Rebecca now keeps a small notebook for new orders. She is very organized the way she records the name of the buyer, the pattern desired, the date that box will be delivered, and the amount and type of payment received. In less than two months, Rebecca has more orders than they can fill in a month. She also brings home some news.

"I am out of a job," she says, on the verge of tears. "Fired! Disgraced in front of the others! Required to leave without reference for taking bandbox orders on company time. And Mrs. Hathaway says no job, no room. Now what will we do?"

"Oh, Rebecca!" comforts Hannah. "*This* is your job now! You have a job right at home with Papa and me. We can send the boxes on the stagecoach, and you can stay at home again."

That Monday morning, when the early signal sounds, Rebecca pulls the covers over her head, and they all sleep soundly till they hear Papa whistling.

# Hannah
## the Bandbox Maker

At first, they worry that when the last bandbox order is filled, Papa will have to find a job or Rebecca will have to return to Lowell. But that never happens. It does not take long for word to spread about Hannah and her wonderful bandboxes. The orders come from working girls by letter and by word. For only five pennies, a girl can trade her sorrowful sack for a genuine bandbox of original design. Orders come from husbands and fathers who want their wives and daughters to travel more suitably. Day in and day out, customers stop by on their way through to choose a box or place an order.

Rebecca is the manager. When she is not minding

the children and the home chores, she keeps track of the orders and lets the customers know when their bandboxes will be ready. She sees to it that the payment is collected—coins or barter.

So far, Rebecca has collected an amazing number of coins, plus one pig, two chickens, a Sunday-best hat, sacks of sugar and flour, a paper of pins, and several yards of homespun.

Soon the shed is filled with boxes of every description. A customer has a choice of splendid colors and patterns. There are cages of songbirds or strutting peacocks; magical forests and flowers of every description; gentle deer or strange beasts of some foreign land; royal lords and ladies dressed for banquets and dances. There are stacks upon stacks of boxes that nearly hit the ceiling.

Hannah and Papa make most of the bandboxes together, and each one seems stronger and prettier than the one before.

"I once scoffed at your fancy notions and thought you were a dreamer," says Papa one day as they work. "And you *are* a dreamer, but you are also capable and clever, and you make your dreams come true."

Treasuring Papa's words, Hannah finds time at the end of the long day to make plans for new boxes, boxes for every use one can imagine. Soon there are comb boxes and collar boxes, gaily decorated with charming small patterns. Next come trinket and glove boxes covered in dogwood or daisies.

One day Hannah decides that if they are a business, they should make themselves known. She fashions a trade sign in the shape of the original bandbox and hangs it outside next to the creaky shed door. It says, simply, BANDBOX MAKER.

And inside the top of each box, Hannah pastes a neatly printed trade card that reads:

---

BAND AND FANCY BOXES
*of every description
made and sold
by
Hannah the Bandbox Maker
Massachusetts*

---

At first, Hannah wants to include Papa's and Rebecca's names on the sign and trade cards, but they agree that it was Hannah's idea that brought them to this new place in their lives, and the credit should be hers alone.

Soon their bandbox business is a year old. Papa still works from sunup till sundown. Now Rebecca is seeing a gentleman from Boston who came by to purchase a bandbox and caught sight of Rebecca. When he

BANDBOX MAKER

BAND & FANCY BOXES
of every description
made and sold by
Hannah the Bandbox Maker
MASSACHUSETTS

learned the story of the bandboxes, he declared that Rebecca would be a lady even with the most tattered sack, which pleased Rebecca.

Maggie now makes mischief in the flour bin with a little coaxing from Sadie and Nora, who are trying harder to keep track of their shoes.

Now Hannah sometimes travels to Lowell with Rebecca to deliver boxes and take new orders. When she does, she uses their box money to bring home fashionable store-bought clothes. When Papa meets them at the depot at the end of a long day, he knows he can cheer up Hannah by exclaiming, "Why, you look like you just stepped out of a bandbox!"

Late one night, Hannah pastes her trade cards inside some new boxes. She does this because it is the style, and because she is proud and hopeful that her boxes will be remembered for a very long time.

## ABOUT THIS BOOK

Today no one bothers to think much about hat-boxes. We just toss our warm knitted hats or baseball caps on the top shelf of the closet, or we hang them on hooks by the door. During mid-nineteenth America, women and men—both young and old—showed respect by wearing a proper hat. And those proper hats, many of them large and stiff, needed a special place for safekeeping. That's why hatboxes were so important then.

Some of the earliest hatboxes were invented by a woman named Hannah Davis who lived in New Hampshire. I learned about Hannah Davis when I visited the Shelburne Museum in Vermont, where some of her beautiful boxes are displayed. I have borrowed a patchwork of facts about this nineteenth-century box-maker to write *Hannah's Fancy Notions*. Like the young girl in my story, also called Hannah, Miss Davis had to support herself. She learned to work with wood from her father, who made clocks, and from her grandfather, who had been a millwright and woodworker. Finally, she found a way to make sturdy wooden hatboxes, and covered them with pretty wallpaper.

Hannah Davis sold many of her hatboxes, or bandboxes, as they were also called, to the young women who worked in nearby textile mills. This was a willing market. Large numbers of girls had to work outside the home to help their families or to support themselves. Many—like the older sister of this story—saved all their wages and sent them home. Others saved every penny for a wedding dowry. But many more were willing and able to spend a part of their wages ($1.85 to $3.00 per week) for pretty and stylish hats and clothing. These new belongings fit perfectly into bandboxes like those Hannah Davis made! Costing twelve to fifty cents, these bright and roomy boxes could be used for storage in their boarding-house sleeping rooms, or as sturdy "suitcases" for occasional visits home.

In their quest for wages and independence, Hannah Davis and the many mill girls became members of the first female industrial labor force. Today we can admire their spunk and their courage. We can also admire the collections of remarkable bandboxes that have been saved, and experience firsthand a small part of women's history.

P.R.

I have borrowed a patchwork of facts about nine-teenth-century band and fancy boxes and about one known bandbox maker, Hannah Davis, who inspired the name of the ten-year-old Hannah of my story.

A brief biographical sketch in *Hat Boxes and Bandboxes at the Shelburne Museum,* published by the Shelburne Museum, tells about Hannah Davis of Jaffrey, New Hampshire, known as "Aunt Hannah," whose resourcefulness resulted in a thriving bandbox business. A number of her handsome wooden bandboxes still exist today at the Shelburne Museum and in private collections.

P.R.